For my dad, Michael, and my dog, Ben

The publisher would like to thank Charlie and Sue Riches for all their help in producing this book.

Copyright © 2007 by Chicken House · Text, initial artwork, and design © 2007 by Annabel Tellis
Finished artwork © 2007 by Ian Butterworth · Dog photography © 2007 by Tracy Morgan

First published in the United Kingdom in 2007 by Chicken House,
2 Palmer Street, Frome, Somerset BA 11 1DS. www.doublecluck.com

Book design by Ian Butterworth and Leyah Jensen

Library of Congress Cataloging-in-Publication Data available · Reinforced Binding for Library Use

Publisher's Note: Although the child in this book has a lot of fun feeding the dog
all sorts of things you wouldn't normally feed a dog, remember this is a work of fiction and
you shouldn't try to feed these same things to your dog—stick with pet food!

ISBN 13: 978-0-439-91387-4 · ISBN 10: 0-439-91387-X
10 9 8 7 6 5 4 3 2 1   07 08 09 10 11

Printed in Singapore · First American edition, May 2007

IF MY DAD WERE A DOG

y Annabel Teilis

Chicken House

Scholastic Inc./New York

If my dad were a dog, just for a day,

I'd tell him to **sit**

and I'd tell him to **stay**.

I'd show him a swing

and a slide that I've seen

and I'd
teach him
    to dance
like a
     butterfly
queen.

I'd buy him a basket and small scoop to use

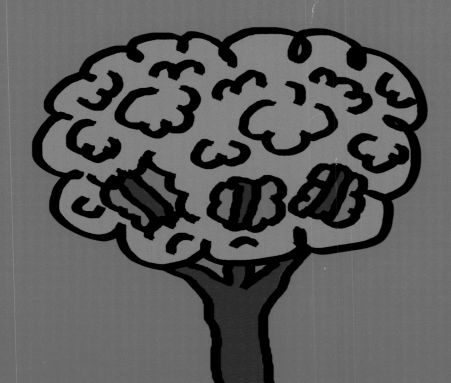

when we've been on our walks

and
he's done
daddy-
doos.

We'd go to a dog show; he'd definitely win

and we'd use his new **trophy** to keep dog treats in.

your DAD won

I'd feed him on muffins and fish fingers with peas;

he'd like raspberry jelly and spaghetti with cheese.

I might let him borrow my polka-dot dish

and I'd
give him
a mint

when his
breath
smells
of fish.

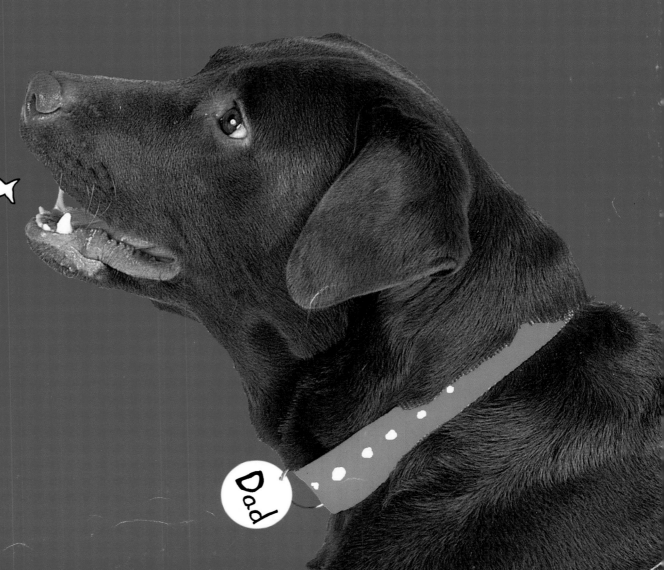

He'd stop for
a drink on the way
to the park.

He'd walk there
so quietly . . .

"Dad, sit down! Dad, that's enough."

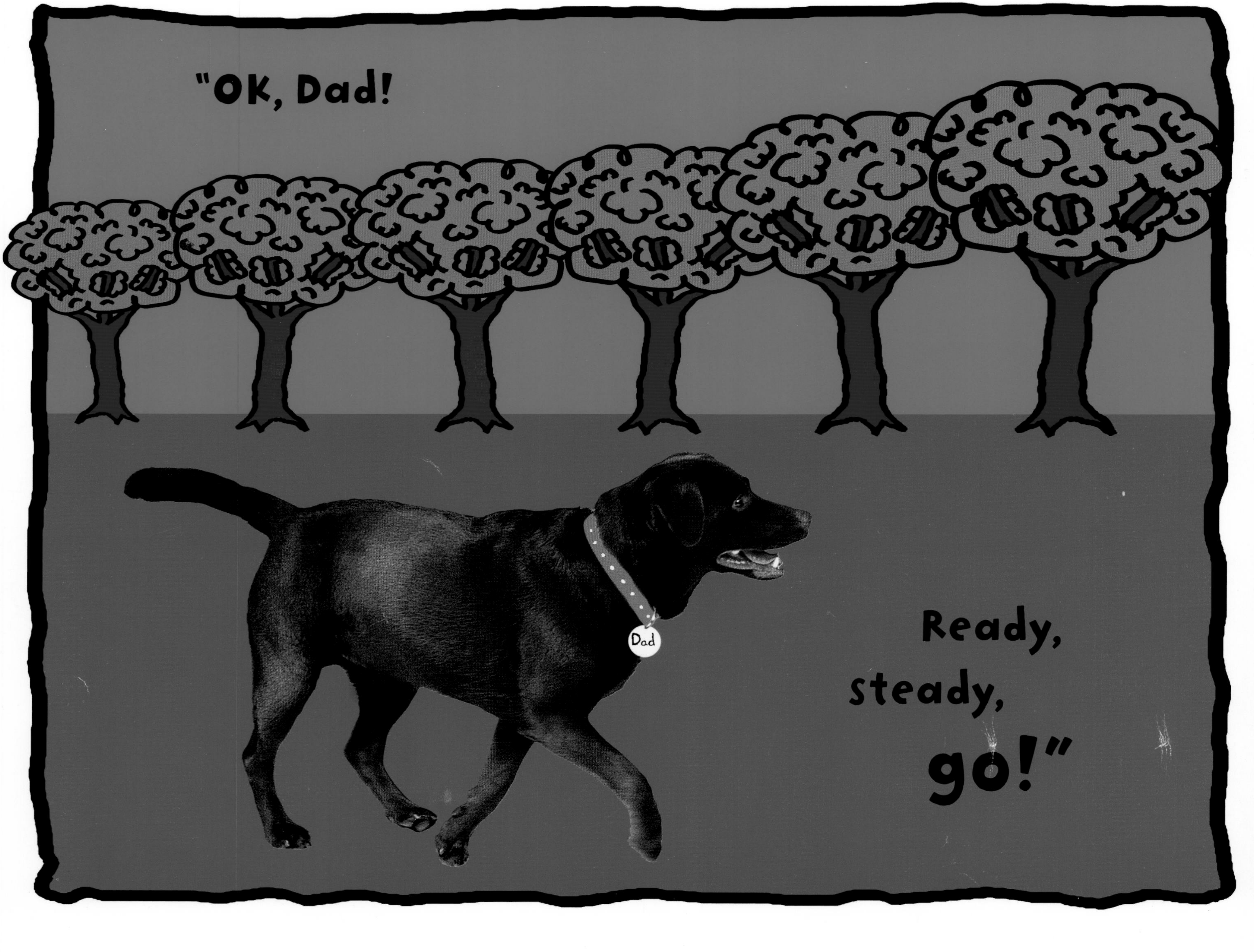

"OK, Dad!

Ready,
steady,
go!"

Woof

Woof

Woof

Woof

Woof

He'd run up to people whom he thinks he knows.
He kisses and
hugs them,
then . . .

Dad

again off he goes.

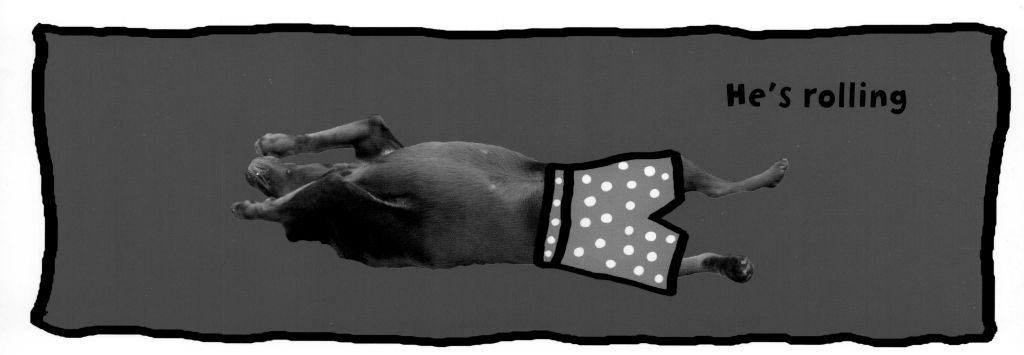

He's rolling

and racing

and sprinkling the flowers.

I manage to catch him

but it takes me four hours.

"Come on, Dad! Let's go home."

"Good Daddy,"
I'd say.

If my dad were a dog,
just for a day.